This sparkling Annual belongs to:

Shannon

Stark

Emma Thomson's
felicity Wishes

FELICITY WISHES
Annual 2006
by Emma Thomson

British Library Cataloguing in Publication Data
A catalogue record of this book is available from the British Library
ISBN 0340 88457
Felicity Wishes © 2000 Emma Thomson. Licensed by White Lion Publishing.
Felicity Wishes Annual 2006 © 2005 Emma Thomson
'Fashion Fiasco', 'Wand Wishes' and 'Dancing Dreams' published in Felicity Wishes Big Book of Magical Mishaps © 2004 Emma Thomson and Helen Bailey

The right of Emma Thomson to be identified as the author and illustrator of this Work
has been asserted by WLP in accordance with the Copyright, Designs and Patents Act 1988.

First edition published 2005
2 4 6 8 10 9 7 5 3 1

Published by Hodder Children's Books, a division of Hodder Headline Limited,
338 Euston Road, London, NW1 3BH

Printed in China

Emma Thomson's felicity Wishes®

Annual 2006

Hodder
Children's
Books

A division of Hodder Headline Limited

Contents

Enter the magical world of

felicity Wishes®

Loves to dance • Sociable and stylish • Her favourite colour is pink • Lives in Little Blossoming • Likes sticky buns • Hopes to be a Friendship Fairy •

Fairy Friends

Felicity Wishes has lots of fairy friends but likes to spend most of her time gossiping and giggling with Holly, Polly and Daisy.

Fairy flying class

Magical makeovers

Dancing to their hearts' content

Gossiping and giggling in the warm summer sun

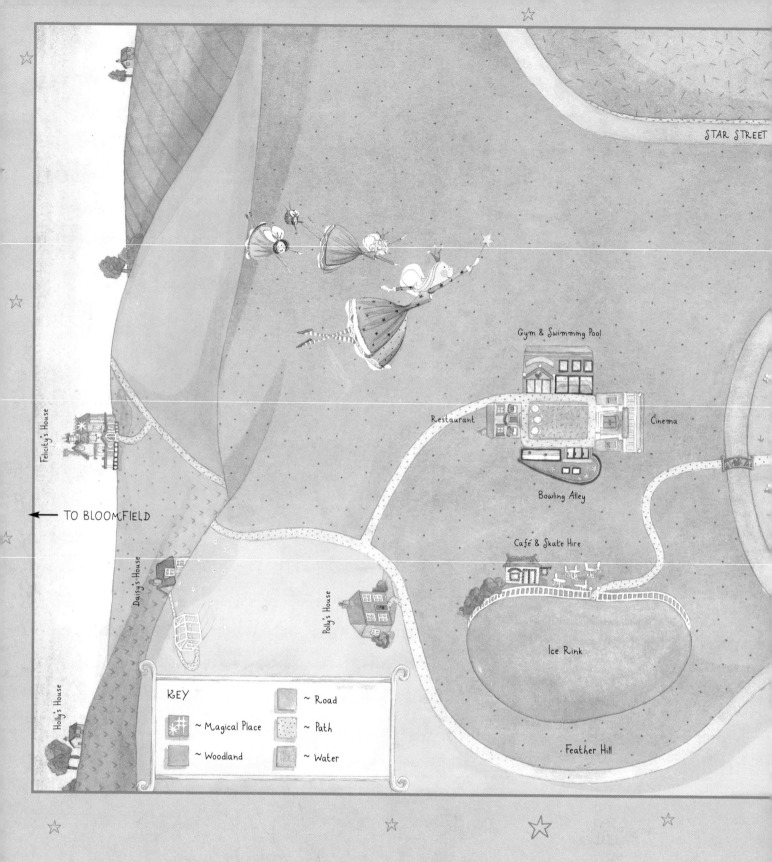

STAR STREET

Gym & Swimming Pool

Restaurant

Cinema

Bowling Alley

Felicity's House

TO BLOOMFIELD

Café & Skate Hire

Daisy's House

Polly's House

Ice Rink

Holly's House

KEY

⊞ ~ Magical Place

■ ~ Road

⠿ ~ Path

■ ~ Woodland

■ ~ Water

Feather Hill

Little Blossoming

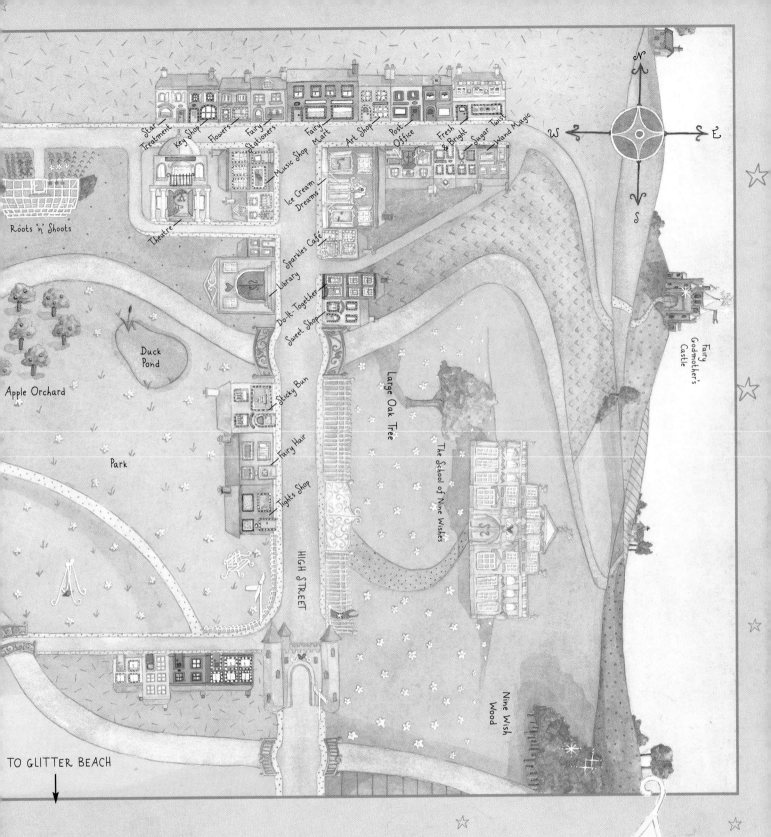

Little Blossoming is a magical place with lots of lovely things to do. Can you find Felicity's house? Where is Sparkles, the café? Can you spot the School of Nine Wishes? Where is Nine Wish Wood?

Close your eyes and visit the place where dreams come true. Wish!

Star Street Shopping

1.

2.

3.

4.

5.

It's a busy day on Star Street in Little Blossoming and fairies everywhere are shopping. Look carefully at this picture – which of the little pictures can you see in the big one?

6.

7.

8.

ANSWERS: ONE, TWO, THREE, FIVE, EIGHT

Fashion Fiasco

Felicity Wishes was having a lovely, lazy morning flicking through the latest copy of *Fairy Girl* magazine. There were lots of really pretty dresses and loads of interesting articles, but the one that had caught her eye was called: 'A Brand New Outfit Equals A Brand New You!' After reading the article, Felicity decided it was time to update her wardrobe.

***

Excitedly, Felicity arrived at Miss Fairy, described in her magazine as 'the top shopping experience for the fashion-conscious fairy'.

But, instead of row upon row of brightly-coloured

dresses, just a few dark-coloured dresses hung in the shadows on matt black rails. It all seemed quite cold and unfriendly, but this was nothing compared to the fairy assistant.

"Can I help you?" said the assistant in a voice which made Felicity think the *last* thing she wanted to do was help.

Shyly, Felicity smoothed down the folds in her skirt, looked up and said as bravely as she could, "I like the dress in the window, but do you have it in pink?"

"We're not stocking *any* pink this year," said the assistant dramatically. "This year, black is the new pink."

Felicity really wanted pink – lilac at a pinch. What was the point of treating yourself to a special outfit if you couldn't buy it in the colour you wanted?

Then she remembered the pictures of the black dresses in *Fairy Girl*. Perhaps it *was* time to try something different. "I'll take this one!"

Felicity didn't feel as skippy and bubbly as she normally did after buying a new dress. In fact, she felt rather flat. It wasn't quite the dress she wanted and it *certainly* wasn't the colour she'd dreamed of. Still, at least she would be at the height of fashion!

***

Felicity unwrapped the dress as soon as she got home. It was very long and very black. Felicity looked at the picture in *Fairy Girl* and then back at her reflection in the mirror.

The dress looked beautiful, elegant and chic in the magazine but on Felicity it looked – and felt – very uncomfortable.

Suddenly, the doorbell chimed. Felicity found she couldn't even walk to the door. Her dress was so long and narrow she had to jump up and down as if she were on a pogo stick.

The doorbell rang again. When Felicity finally opened the door, Polly, Holly and Daisy stared at their friend for a moment before collapsing with laughter.

"What ARE you wearing?" asked Polly, her eyes streaming with tears.

"Are you off to a fancy dress party?" enquired Holly

between fits of giggles.

So Felicity explained about seeing the dress in *Fairy Girl* and how she wanted to be a fashionable fairy on the move, but now she was a fashionable fairy who couldn't move and she really didn't like the new Felicity as much as the old one.

Daisy came over to Felicity and hugged her tightly. "Felicity," she said, "we love you just the way you are. We don't want a new Felicity, we like the old one!"

"It's what's on the inside that counts, not the outside!" added Polly.

"What am I going to do with this dress?" said Felicity, looking at her very black and very straight dress.

"We'll have to take it back tomorrow," said Daisy. "I'm sure there won't be a problem. In the meantime, you have five minutes to get out of that black dress and into your favourite pink dress and then we'll all go out for an ice cream!"

Cake Crisis

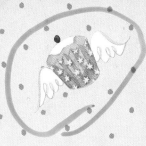

Felicity Wishes always tries as hard as she can
at school. But in cookery class her fairy cakes
are so light they float away!
How many cakes can you find?

Bake
a fairy cake and
wish all your
worries away.

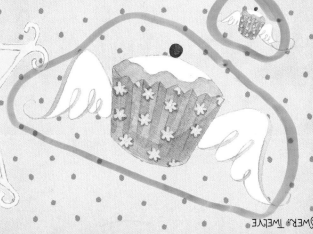

Dramatic Dilemma

Everywhere is covered with snow and Felicity can't find
her way home. Follow the snowflakes and help Felicity fly there.

Home

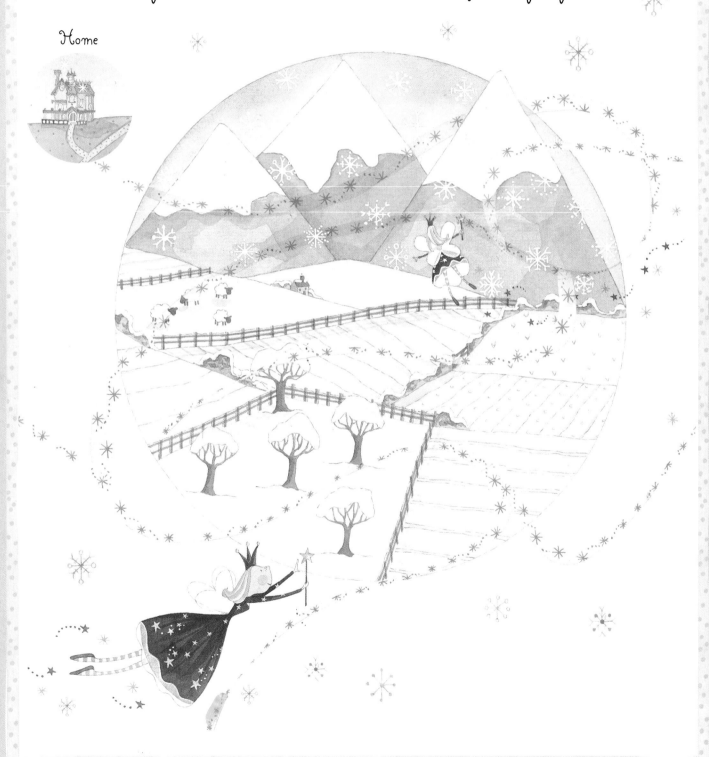

Wand Worry

Felicity Wishes has lost her wand and is frantically flying around Little Blossoming, trying to find it. You will need a counter for each player and a dice.

Start 1

2

3

Stop for an emergency break. Miss a go. **4**

Stop for a gossip. Go back three spaces. **15**

14

Oops! You've taken a wrong turn. Miss a go. **13**

16

A gush of wind blows you to 19. **17**

5

6

Have forty winks.
Go back two spaces.
7

8

12

Cartwheel forwards.
three spaces.
11

Phone a friend for their
advice. Have another go.
9

10

Make a wish
to find your wand.
Move to 19.
18

19

Finish
20

Snowball Surprise

Felicity Wishes is enjoying winter until she is ambushed with a snowball! Can you put these photographs in order?

Fairy Find

Felicity is flying over Little Blossoming trying to find her fairy friends.
But where are they? Start at square one, move four squares to the right,
three down, and one to the right. Can you see them?

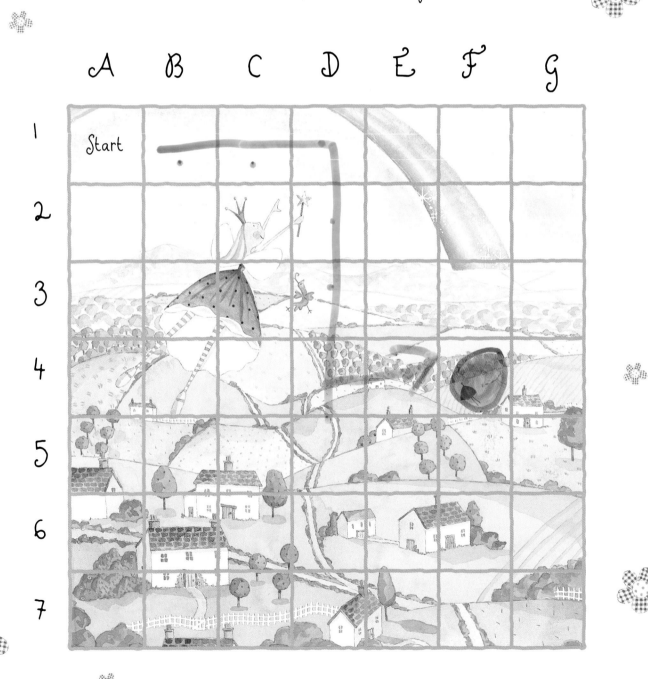

Flying Fun

Felicity Wishes and her fairy friends know that practice
makes perfect, especially when it comes to flying.
Join in the fun and copy the fairy moves!

Double loop
twist

Sparkle spin

Backwards flip

Two legged leap

Point your wand

Head for the stars

Triple twist take-off

Try to make your wishes come true by really believing in your dreams.

Birthday Bonanza

Holly, Polly and Daisy have arranged a surprise birthday party at Ice Cream Dreams for Felicity.

Spread a little sparkle and make wishes for all your friends.

1. How many wands are there? **9**

2. Are there four or five ice cream cones in the picture? **4**

3. How many sets of wings can you see? **12**

4. How many party invitations can you find? **2**

Dainty Differences

Felicity and Holly meet in their favourite place under the Large Oak Tree for a gossip and a giggle. Can you spot the six differences between these two pictures?

Make a friendship wish for your very best friend.

ANSWERS: APPLE, CROWN, BOOK, BIRD, CARD, HOLLY'S DRESS

Wand Wishes

The bell for first break rang. Felicity Wishes and her best friends, Polly, Holly and Daisy, flew as fast as they could to get to the sunniest spot on the playing field before anyone else.

They were halfway there, when Felicity remembered she'd left her wand behind.

"I must have left it in the hall," sighed Felicity. "I'll go to lost property after school and see if anyone's handed it in."

"You can't go a whole day without your wand!" cried Holly in disbelief. "You're a fairy!"

"It'll be all right," she said. "I'm sure we won't have to practise granting wishes today."

***

But it *wasn't* all right. In geography, Felicity was asked to point out all the countries on the globe that began with the letter A, but she had nothing to point with. In music class, it was her turn to conduct the recorders, so she had to do it with her finger, and everyone ended up playing at different times – and in art class they were asked to trace round their wands to make a picture!

By the time the last lesson was over, Felicity was desperate for her wand. She'd never realised how much she needed it. Wands weren't just for making wishes, they were handy for all *sorts* of things.

***

"Have you had any wands handed in?" Felicity asked the Lost Property Fairy, Miss Sing.

"Sorry, dear, no. In fact, in all my years as a Lost Property Fairy, I've *never* had a wand handed in!"

"Oh," said Felicity quietly, looking down at her toes.

"It's not the sort of thing a fairy normally loses," explained Miss Sing.

"I know," said Felicity, beginning to feel rather sad. "I don't think I'll *ever* make a proper fairy."

"Why don't you go to the new wand shop, Wand Magic?" said Miss Sing.

Feeling instantly perkier, Felicity flew off in the direction of the shops. Shopping, it has to be said, was one of Felicity's favourite things.

✳✳✳

Wand Magic in Little Blossoming had only been open for a few days, but already it was said to be the best fairy wand shop for miles. Even before you reached it, you could see the pavement outside glittering. Each hand-made wand was displayed in a glass case, on a deep pink velvet cushion with gold trimming.

Felicity stood in the doorway, her mouth wide-open in wonder.

"Can I help?" asked the friendly assistant.

"I'd like a new wand, please," said Felicity eagerly. "Something that I would want to look after properly."

"Well," said the assistant clapping her hands, "today is your lucky day! We've just had a delivery of… THESE!"

Felicity gasped. "They're beautiful!"

"Breathtaking, aren't they? I guarantee you'll be the only fairy in Little Blossoming with a silver starred wand, which really *is* special!"

Felicity literally danced out of the wand shop – and she danced all the way home too, waving her silver starred wand as she went.

✳✳✳

There wasn't a fairy at the School of Nine Wishes who hadn't heard about Felicity's wand by the time she arrived the next day.

"It's beautiful," sighed Polly. "My gold wand looks so dowdy in comparison."

"It's just too sparkly for words," said Daisy, putting a hand over her eyes.

"It's stunning," said Holly reluctantly. Holly always prided herself on being the trendiest fairy but Felicity had beaten her to it this time.

Felicity smiled. "It didn't seem quite right that I was the only one with a silver starred wand so I went back to the shop and bought three more – one for each of you!"

"Really?" said the fairy friends, suddenly cheering up.

"Really," said Felicity, handing over the sparkly wands. "Come on, let's practise making wishes with our new wands."

Star Treatment

1. What is Felicity holding in her hand?

2. What colour are the hairdressers' dresses?

3. What is the pattern on Felicity's tights?

4. What is the name of the magazine?

5. How many biscuits are in the picture?

6. Who is having her hair styled?

Sparkly make-up and magic hair mousse – treat yourself!

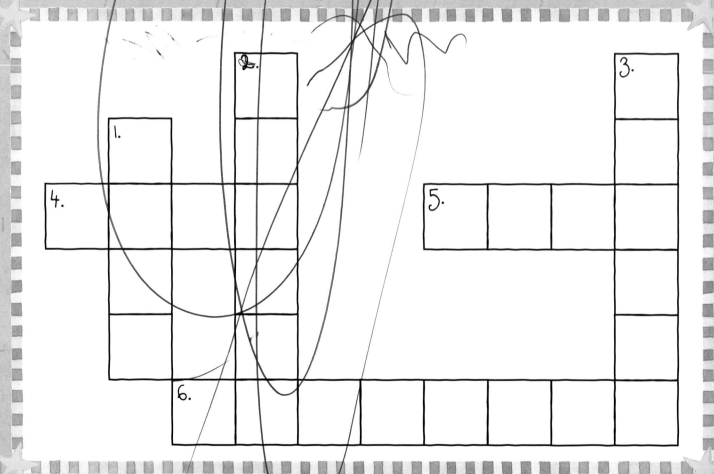

ANSWERS: 1. WAND 2. PURPLE 3. STRIPY 4. HAIR 5. FOUR 6. FELICITY

Special Stars

Wish on a star and watch it twinkle to make your wish come true.

Felicity Wishes is catching extra-special stars for each of her fairy friends. How many stars has she caught? How many are left to catch?

ANSWER: 1. THREE 2. EIGHT

Favourite Fairy

Felicity Wishes is
everyone's favourite friend. Join the
dots and add a little dazzle to this picture.

Dress Drama

Felicity Wishes has bought a new dress for the Fairy Ball. Which two pictures are the same?

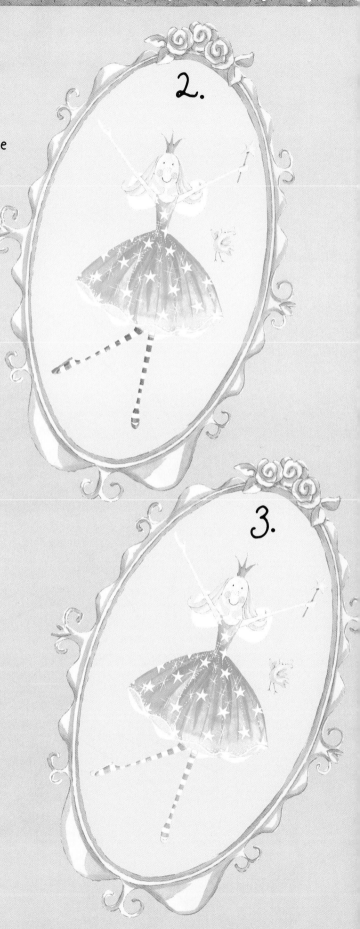

Put on your brightest dress and make a colourful, sparkly wish.

4.

5.

6.

7.

ANSWER: ONE AND THREE

Magical Moon

Felicity Wishes can't sleep as the moonlight is shining through her bedroom window. Can you find her magazine, keys and wand?

Floury Fairies

Felicity and her friends have been trying to follow Jenny Olivia's recipe for a perfect fairy cake. The fairies are covered in flour! Can you work out who is behind the flour?

1.

2.

3.

4.

Spring Surprise

Spring has sprung in Little Blossoming and all the fairies are enjoying the warm weather.

1. How many fairies can you see?

2. Are there seven or eight rabbits in this scene?

3. How many wands can you find?

4. How many butterflies can you see?

5. Can you find the snail?

43

Winter Wonderland

Felicity and her friends have enjoyed all the fun of winter. Unscramble these photographs and complete the wintry scenes.

Sparkling Spa

Felicity is flying to Holly's house for a fairy spa day. She's carrying bags and bags of beauty products but has dropped some items along the way. Can you find the correct way?

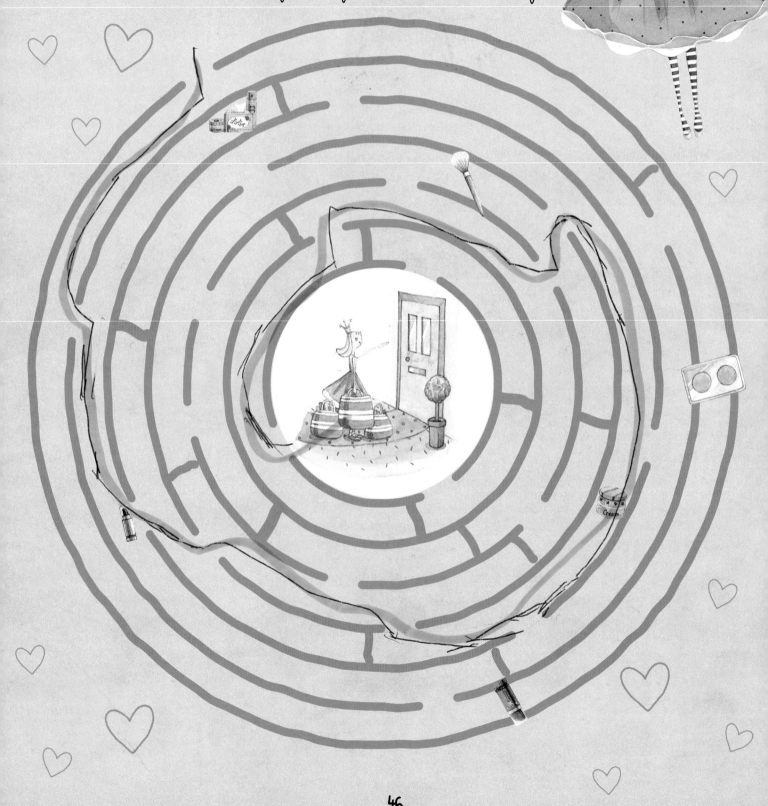

Pretty Presents

Felicity Wishes loves to buy presents for all her fairy friends. Join in the fun and add a little sparkle to this picture.

Secrets and Surprises

It's nearly Felicity's birthday and she's preparing for her party. Can you put the pictures in the right order to show the story?

1. First Felicity wrote sparkly invitations to all of her fairy friends.

2. Next on her list of things to do was to buy a pair of new stripy tights.

3. Then she treated herself to a funky new hairstyle at Fairy Hair.

4. Afterwards, Polly invited Felicity to Ice Cream Dreams for a special treat but it was closed!

5. Felicity opened the door to find a surprise birthday party just for her!

Make this
the day for lots
of fun wishes!

Diamond Dancer

Felicity Wishes is learning some new dance routines. Help her complete each sequence by drawing the correct picture in the space.

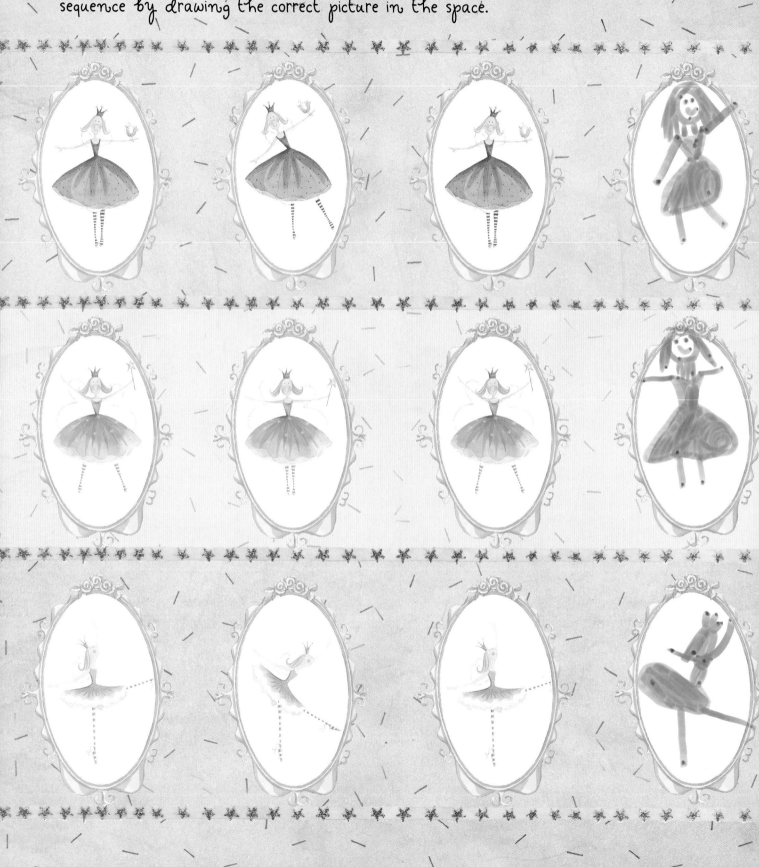

Perfect Puzzle

Felicity Wishes and her fairy friends are making lots of
magical things in sewing class.
Can you help complete this scene?

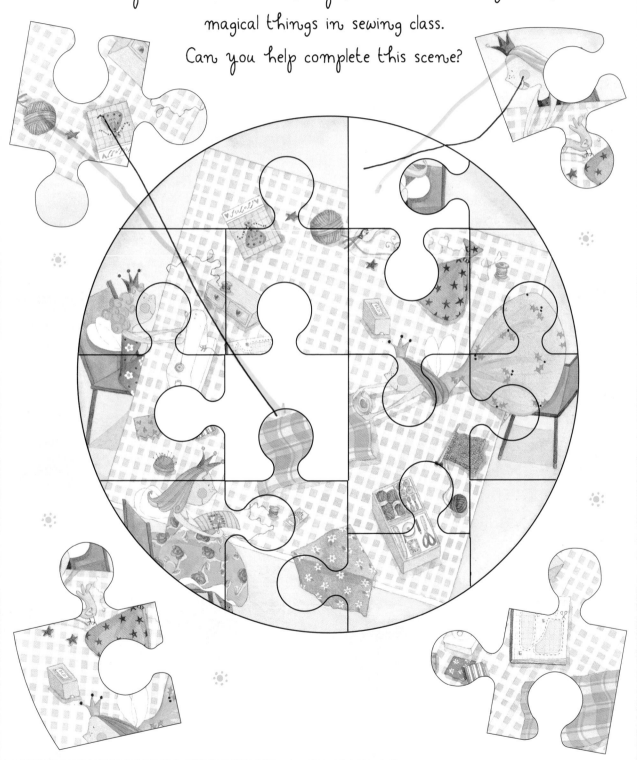

Dancing Dreams

A trip to the ballet had been arranged for the students of Madame Plié's Dancing School to see a performance of *Swan Lake*. Everyone was very excited – no one more so than Felicity Wishes. Everything about going to the ballet made her tingle with excitement: the sound of the orchestra tuning up, the muffled chatter of the crowd waiting for the performance to begin, the seats with their plump red velvet cushions, but most of all, the thought of what lay behind the large red velvet curtains.

From the first pirouette, Felicity thought *Swan Lake* was the most wonderful ballet she had ever seen and Natasha Milletova the most beautiful ballerina imaginable. Her wing control was astounding. She could fly across the stage effortlessly, her wings barely appearing to move.

She swooped and dived and hovered and spun with

breathtaking grace and ease, her tiny silver ballet shoes twinkling magically under the lights. No wonder it was rumoured that she dipped her feet in a tray of magic dust before a performance.

When the curtain finally came down at the end of the performance, the audience rose to their feet and cheered. Felicity tried to whistle but Madame gave her a stern look, so she stood on tiptoe and waved as hard as she could.

On Saturday morning, the fairies gathered at the dancing school. Most of them were still chattering about *Swan Lake*, but Felicity was still dreaming about it. If only she could dance as well as Natasha.

Holly, Polly, Daisy and the other fairies carefully followed Madame Plié's instructions, but Felicity was too busy dreaming about *Swan Lake*. Although she started in first position she was still in it when the others had moved on to fourth!

Finally, the class came to an end. Tutus, tights and shoes were packed away and the class began to empty.

When everyone had gone, Felicity began to dance, pretending that she was Natasha. Faster and faster she danced, throwing herself around the room. She attempted a mid-air pirouette, but lost her bearings and landed on the chandelier hanging from the ceiling.

What on earth was Felicity going to do? All her friends had left to go to Sparkles and Madame Plié was nowhere to be seen. She could be here all night!

After what seemed like hours, the door opened and in walked a tiny figure wearing woolly socks and a woolly jumper over a pair of grey tights.

Felicity was about to shout "HELP!" when she realised that the fairy was none other than Natasha Milletova.

To Felicity's amazement, Natasha walked to the centre of the room and began to practise the same amazing arabesques and perfect pirouettes that Felicity and her friends had seen on stage.

Suddenly, Felicity's nose began to twitch. The chandelier was very dusty.

"ATISHOO!" Felicity sneezed hard.

Natasha looked up sharply at the young fairy hanging helplessly from the light.

"Are you all right?" enquired the Prima Ballerina as she quickly flew up to Felicity and untangled her wings.

Felicity blushed. She started to tell Natasha that after seeing *Swan Lake* she had been daydreaming in her ballet class about being her, and then she had got carried away.

"Thank you so much for helping me," said Felicity.

Natasha reached into her bag and, after some searching, pulled out a pair of tiny, pink ballet shoes, which she handed to Felicity. Felicity was speechless.

"Now off you go, so I can practise. I'm sure I'll see you again soon."

Felicity hardly heard her, she was so busy saying thank you. Then she flew as fast as she could to Sparkles and showed her friends the tiny pink shoes.

"There's something tucked inside," said Holly, peering at them closely.

Felicity reached in and pulled out four tickets for that evening's performance of *The Nutcracker*. It was only then that she remembered Natasha's parting words. She really *would* be seeing her again soon!

Fairy Fashion

Felicity Wishes has won a free photo-shoot with Fairy Girl magazine. There's lots to do before the shoot – will she make it on time? You will need a dice and one counter for each player.

4

Can't decide what to wear. Miss a go.

1 Start

2

3

14

16

Polly lends you a bag to match your outfit. Flutter to 19.

7

15

18

Daisy gives you her magical shampoo recipe. Fly to 21.

19

Relax with a cucumber eye mask. Go forwards two spaces.

20

21

5

6
Lost your invitation.
Go back three spaces.

Fairy Fashion Invitation
Felicity Wishes
is invited to a
free photo-shoot

7

8
Stop to buy a new pair
of shoes. Go back
three spaces.

13
Find your dry-
cleaning ticket for
your favourite
dress. Fly to 15.

12

11
Your make-
up doesn't go
to plan.
Miss a go.

10

9

22

23

24
Finish

Messy Muddle

Felicity Wishes can never find
anything in her messy bedroom.
Help Felicity find her lost items
in the wordsearch below.

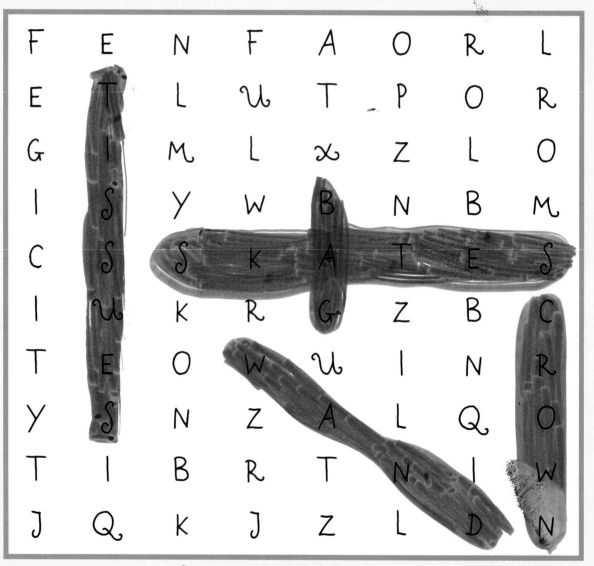

F	E	N	F	A	O	R	L			L
E	T	L	U	T	P	O	R			R
G	I	M	L	x	Z	L			O	
I	S	Y	W	B	N	B			M	
C	S	S	K	A	T	E			S	
I	U	K	R	G	Z	B			C	
T	E	O	W	U	I	N			R	
Y	S	N	Z	A	L	Q			O	
T	I	B	R	T	N	I			W	
J	Q	K	J	Z	L	D			N	

skates   tissues   crown   wand   bag

Fairy Star Biscuits

350g (12oz) plain flour

100g (4oz) butter

1 medium egg

175g (6oz) soft brown sugar

2 teaspoons of bicarbonate of soda

2 teaspoons of ginger

4 tablespoons of golden syrup

Pre-heat the oven to 180°C/350°F /Gas 4. Cream the butter and sugar together until light and fluffy and then beat in the egg with one tablespoon of flour and add the bicarbonate of soda.

Add the ginger and syrup and fold in the remaining flour. Line a bun tin with paper cases and half fill each case with the mixture. Bake in the oven for about 20 minutes. Remove and put on a wire rack to cool before decorating.

Always remember to ask an adult for help when cooking.

Hold this
book in your
hands and close your eyes tight.
Count backwards from ten and when
you reach number one whisper your wish...
...but make sure no one can hear.

Keep this book in a safe
place and, maybe, one day,
your wish just might come true.

Love felicity x